THE TUNNY TUNNELS IN THE TUNNEL

Michael Rex

Ready-to-Read

Simon Spotlight
New York   Amsterdam/Antwerp   London
Toronto   Sydney/Melbourne   New Delhi

SIMON SPOTLIGHT • An imprint of Simon & Schuster Children's Publishing Division
1230 Avenue of the Americas, New York, New York 10020
This Simon Spotlight edition July 2025 • Text and illustrations © 2025 by Michael Rex
All rights reserved, including the right of reproduction in whole or in part in any form. SIMON SPOTLIGHT, READY-TO-READ, and colophon are registered trademarks of Simon & Schuster, LLC. • For information about special discounts for bulk purchases, please contact Simon & Schuster Special Sales at 1-866-506-1949 or business@simonandschuster.com. • The Simon & Schuster Speakers Bureau can bring authors to your live event. For more information or to book an event contact the Simon & Schuster Speakers Bureau at 1-866-248-3049 or visit our website at www.simonspeakers.com.
Manufactured in the United States of America 0325 LAK • 10 9 8 7 6 5 4 3 2 1
Library of Congress Cataloging-in-Publication Data | Names: Rex, Michael, author, illustrator. | Title: The tunneler tunnels in the tunnel / by Michael Rex. | Description: Simon Spotlight edition. | New York : Simon Spotlight, 2025. | Series: Ready-to-read. Level 1 | Summary: A penguin in a hardhat digs in a tunnel, popping up in different places, visiting a gardener, a farmer, a banker and others until he and everybody along the way reach a surprise ending. | Identifiers: LCCN 2024018587 (print) | LCCN 2024018588 (ebook) | ISBN 9781665962094 (paperback) | ISBN 9781665962100 (hardcover) | ISBN 9781665962117 (ebook) | Subjects: CYAC: Tunnels—Fiction. | Occupations—Fiction. | LCGFT: Picture books. | Classification: LCC PZ7.R32875 Tu 2025 (print) | LCC PZ7.R32875 (ebook) | DDC [E]—dc23 | LC record available at https://lccn.loc.gov/2024018587

To my sister, Karen

The tunneler tunnels in the tunnel.

The tunneler tunnels in the tunnel.

The shopper shops at the shop.

The tunneler tunnels in the tunnel.

The banker banks at the bank.

The tunneler tunnels in the tunnel.

The tunneler tunnels in the tunnel.

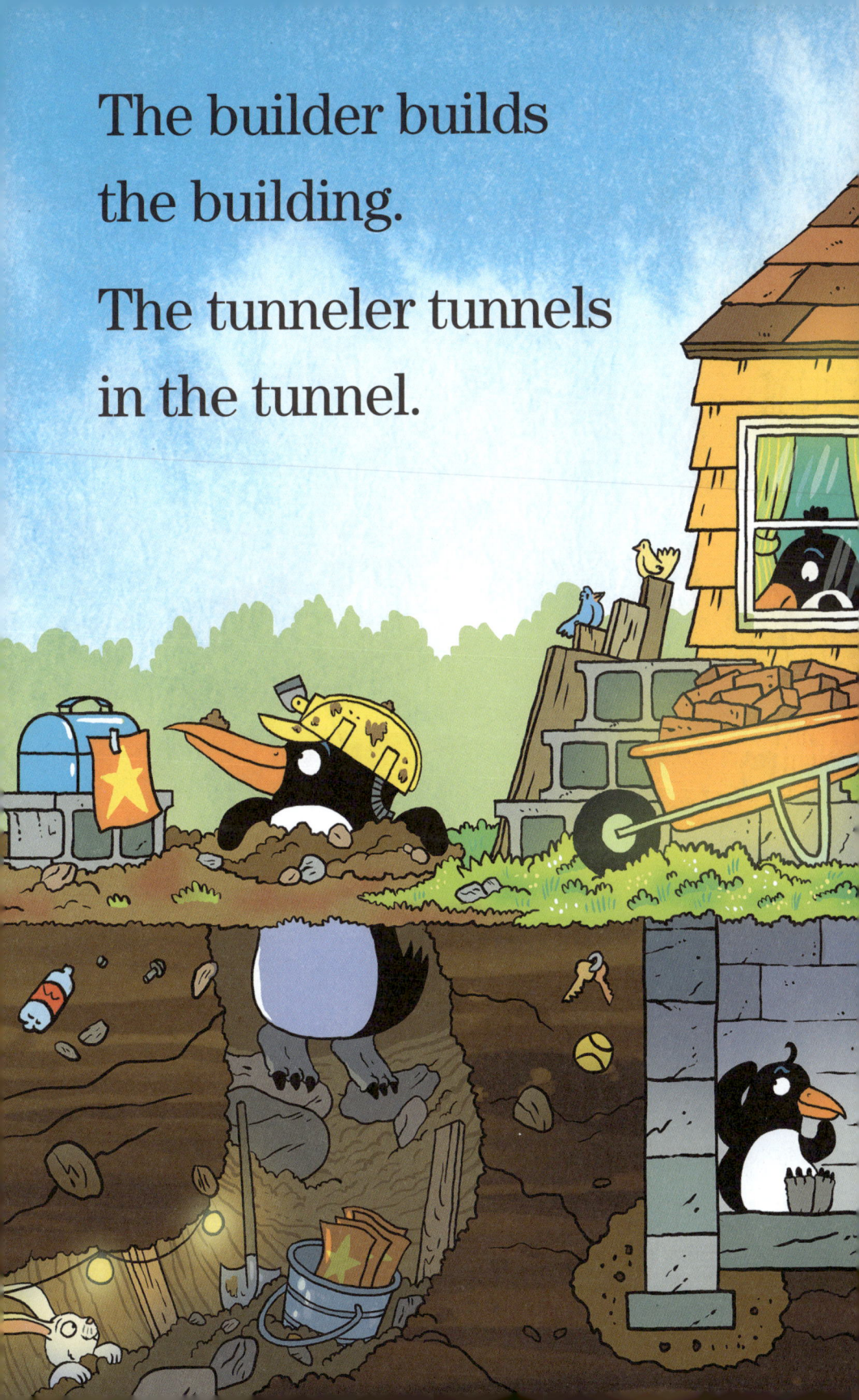

The builder builds the building.

The tunneler tunnels in the tunnel.

The tunneler tunnels in the tunnel.

The hiker hikes on the hike.

The tunneler tunnels in the tunnel.

The tunneler tunnels in the tunnel.

The fielder fields
in the field.

The tunneler tunnels in the tunnel.

The tunneler tunnels in the tunnel.

The dancers dance at the dance!